MAID DIRTY

DIRTY BILLIONAIRE BOSS

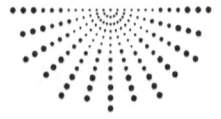

TALA MELTON

plicit Press
Erotica Fiction

GET NAUGHTY UPDATES

Click here or Visit
TalaMelton.com
for more Naughty Maid Stories

eISBN: 978-1-62327-817-5

Print ISBN: 978-1-62327-818-2

CHAPTER ONE

"You're naughty," Landon said to Melissa. He was the chef in billionaire Ivor Springfield's Bel Air mansion, and he had just had another flirtatious encounter with the housekeeper, Melissa. She really didn't mean anything by it, just having a bit of innocent fun. The days running and managing the sprawling estate could be tedious, so she found a way to liven things up a bit.

"You know it," she said, and she walked out of the kitchen, pulling her skirt down unnecessarily.

She did have a tendency to take things a little too far, sometimes flirting with her boss. Ivor read beyond her double entendres and sexual innuendo, though, so he, too, just played along. He enjoyed Melissa, and it did help that she was easy on the eye.

She served him his lunch by the pool. He was sitting alone, reading the day's newspapers. It was a little late, but he had just woken up around noon, so it was acceptable. Wealth was a great remover of needing to do anything at any particular time, so his watch really was just a very expensive timepiece.

"Thank you," he said. He didn't look up at her as she put the tray down, and she didn't move. She set his plate and cutlery in front of him and announced the meal with great ceremony. She seemed to have delusions of working for Buckingham Palace.

"Will you need anything else, sir," she asked.

"No, that will be all..." Ivor said, looking up at her now.

She was standing closer to him than she should have been so that he almost felt like he should move his chair. After a protracted minute, she simply said that she knew where to find her if he needed anything else. "Absolutely anything," she said, as loaded as she could have made the statement.

As she walked away, his eyes lifted towards her. He watched the sexy blonde walk away, letting his mind go briefly to where it really shouldn't. He put down the paper in his hand and set about eating the poached egg on rye that was his lunch.

Melissa really had a way of crossing a line without really crossing it. And even when she went too far, she had a way of bringing it back so that you were left thinking that she was just joking. She usually was, though, which is what made her fun to have around.

"Do you enjoy it," Landon asked?

"What?"

"Being such a tease..."

"Me, a tease, never..." She said while buttoning and unbuttoning just the top button on her housekeeper's uniform.

"It's going to get you in trouble one day..." He said before returning to the preparation of the veal that would be dinner.

"I live for trouble," she winked.

And she really did. Before she found herself in her current job, the 22-year old had been an entertainer of the exotic kind. She enjoyed stripping too, but she realized soon enough that exotic dancer wasn't gonna look good on her resume, not too long anyway. So she swopped lapdances for making beds, and while it was boring as hell, her prospects seemed better.

This was probably where her flirting skills were perfected. It really was amazing what skills one could pick up for the right price. She had fond memories of those days, too, enjoying how easily men were to manipulate.

There was this one time she remembered when it did go a little too far. The "No sex in the champagne room" wasn't just an urban myth. It really was a rule. But this particular gentlemen wanted what was clearly not on offer, and it wasn't, if Melissa was entirely honest with herself, his fault entirely. She had danced upon him, yes, but the suggestive whispers she spoke in his ears were not necessary, but she did it anyway.

He asked for a private dance, which she obliged, of course, the tips were better, and when they were alone in the private booth, his hands went places they shouldn't. She continued to flirt with him even when it was getting aggressive, and before she knew what was happening, it was almost too late to stop him.

Fortunately, security stepped in, and she managed to dodge the proverbial bullet.

Melissa, being Melissa though, met the very same man outside the club, and they went back to his hotel. There they played, and he got everything he wanted, and so did she. It was a night of adult fun that they both enjoyed, but she knew that her looks wouldn't last forever, so she needed a solid plan for her life.

So now she was Ivor Springfield's housekeeper, and for the most part, she enjoyed it. There were enough male members of Ivor's staff to keep her entertained. And Ivor himself, although proving resistant, was also fun to toy with.

She went back down to the swimming pool to get the tray. She found that Ivor had left already, and so she just cleared the table. She also folded the newspapers and took everything inside. After dropping everything in the scullery, she went to her bedroom and took a shower. She was done for the day, knowing that Landon would serve Ivor his dinner.

"You gonna spend the night in," Landon asked.

"Where would you suggest I went?"

"Fuck off; I was just making conversation..." He said, and they both laughed.

CHAPTER TWO

*M*elissa walked into Ivor's study one morning, carrying him a coffee. He hadn't asked for coffee.

"You seem to really like to be around me..." Ivor said.

"I work for you, sir..."

"Put the coffee on the table, and close the door..." he said.

She did as she was told, closing the door and locking it, with her still inside the study. Ivor looked up and shook his head.

"Your instructions weren't clear..." she smiled and turned to unlock the door.

"Keep it locked... And come here..." he said, looking at her curiously. "Do you like to play games?"

"I do... I'm sorry if I offended you..."

"I'm not offended... You like to play... Let's play!"

He was standing in front of her now, Melissa against the door. He pulled down his zipper and pulled himself out. He held his flaccid meat in his hand, using the other hand to push Melissa down onto her knees. She smiled to herself, and when she was face to face with his large head, she opened her mouth and started to suck on it softly.

It hardened quickly, filling her mouth as quickly. She knew she was really just messing with him, but now it seemed that he had beaten her at her own game. She was sucking on his throbbing erection, and there was no turning back. She was also enjoying it, so it really was a win-win situation.

Ivor was holding her head in place, thrusting into her mouth with real verve. He was going to cum in her mouth, and he was determined to see her swallow every drop. He had played her game long enough, and while the flirtation was playful, he needed her to know that there were consequences to her actions.

Melissa was thinking of these consequences too. She thought that she had won, breaking through her boss's defenses. They obviously both had different ideas of what was happening here.

He thrust harder into her mouth, sending himself deep into the back of her throat. He was close now, and so he held her head a little harder. A few more strokes, and he would shoot, he knew. And then the lesson would have been taught.

As he shot into her mouth, he almost fell over, so intense was the orgasm. He held her head, emptying himself into her mouth and watching as she did, in fact, swallow his excessive load.

He pulled himself from her mouth, letting just his head linger a while in her mouth so that she could savor the last few drops. Then he pulled his cock from her and put it away. She remained on her knees as be walked back to his side of the desk. He took a sip of the coffee.

" This is cold... bring me a fresh pot, " he said.

She wiped her mouth and stood up. Straightening her skirt, she took the tray off the table and left the study. Her head was racing; she was wondering if she had pleased him if she could have perhaps done more. There wasn't time; he caught her off guard; she tried to console herself.

When she returned with the fresh cup, he still said nothing. His head was buried in work, and he made no attempt at acknowledging her. She left in silence, feeling more than a little inadequate. She went straight to her bedroom and locked the door, throwing herself on the bed. What had she done wrong, she wondered?

There was nobody she could talk to. There was nobody she could test her oral skills on, nobody she wanted to test them on. She was a master flirt, she knew. But apparently, if this morning's experience was anything to go by, that was all she was good at.

She had never received any complaints before. Nobody had ever said anything negative about her skills. But now, here was the one man she flirted with, the one man she desperately wanted to please, and he was cold and dismissive.

Little did she know that he was playing her at her own game. The billionaire had always won every single game he had ever played, and this would be no different. He just wasn't sure if Melissa would be as keen on flirting with him after this morning.

She was relentless, though; he knew this. So he knew it wouldn't be long before she upped the stakes herself. There was a strange cat and mouse vibe between them. There had been for a while now. The question was, who was the cat and who was the mouse.

"You called, sir," Melissa said when she walked into the study for the second time that day.

"Yes, come in..." He didn't look up, summoning her to him with just his hands.

She stood by the door for a while and then started to walk slowly towards him.

"Lock the door..." He said, again without looking up.

She did and then walked towards the study desk. It was a mahogany monstrosity, so even when she stood on the other side of the table, they were really worlds apart. He didn't stand up. He just pushed his chair back and summoned her around to his side of the table.

She was excited but tried hard not to show it. He wanted more, and that really was all that mattered now. She stood in front of him, and he pushed the chair in just a little, pinning her to the side of the table.

CHAPTER THREE

*H*e lifted her skirt, again not saying a word. Ivor ran his fingers above the rim of her panties; then, he moved just a single finger down directly onto her secret place. It wasn't much of a secret, though, except for the fact that it was still covered in delicate lace.

Ivor used his fingertip to write something on her. Words, maybe numbers, she wasn't sure. She didn't care. It felt incredible.

"You've gotten away with this for a long time..." He said.

"Away with what, exactly," she asked, breathless. She was trying to figure out what he was writing, her focus on the fullness of her bloom, though.

He pulled her panties down to her knees. Then he tapped her directly. She was fully engorged, and with each tap of his finger, her arousal and her clit grew. It was soon as large as it was going to get. And so he stopped tapping, stopped teasing. Instead, he put his finger in his mouth and then slowly inserted it deep inside her.

It went so deep that she had to place her hand on his, to stop him. He stopped moving his finger and then slowly pulled this finger from her. He went in again, quickly. Not so quickly, though, that she felt the need to stop him. This intrusion was moist, which made the intrusion just a little more comfortable.

She held her skirt up and watched as he moved just this finger in and out of her. All in and all out, he fingered her deliciously. He needed to do nothing more. There was absolutely nothing else needed but the wonderful work of this single digit. Ivor had the kind of thick fingers that made fingering worth it.

Melissa closed her eyes now, her hands still on her skirt. The thick digit was bringing her closer and closer, and she loved it. She wanted to be doing something to him too, but she couldn't. Pinned against the table with a finger moving steadily in and out of her was all she could focus on right now.

She was so close now she could scream. And just then, the finger was out of her. He had literally left her hanging. She needed to cum, wanting to bring herself to an end herself now, but she couldn't. Ivor just pulled her panties back up and asked her to get him a drink, saying that he needed to make a phone call.

She almost screamed. If she thought she was good before, she had definitely met her match. He was clearly the master at whatever this was they were doing. But it was what it was, and so she just pulled her skirt down and left the study. Melissa was aching inside, still.

"What would you like to drink?"

"Anything... Now go!"

When she returned, he really was on the phone. She put the drink down on the table and left. She managed to escape before he could if he wanted to, of course, stop her. She went straight into the guest bathroom to finish what Ivor had started.

She pulled her panties down and touched herself. She really touched herself. Her fingers were on her and then inside her. One finger, then two fingers. She dug deep into herself with just these two fingers, and it just wasn't feeling the same. She thought of getting Landon to help her out or any of the other males on staff, but she thought better of it. She would just give it time, confident that she would soon get into her groove.

It wasn't happening, though. The two fingers were not cutting it, and this was probably because she was doing it to herself. She was used to touching herself; she was used to getting herself off. But Ivor had set the bar so high already that there was no way she could match that.

She added a third finger. This got her a little more excited, and so she knew that she might just get it right. If she was in her own bedroom, she knew she would have the time to get it done properly. But she was just doors away from the man who had brought her up only to bring her down again, rather unceremoniously.

Melissa dug into herself hard with the three fingers, really pulling the orgasm that was still pending deep inside her. She could feel it coming, but it definitely wasn't coming fast enough. And she needed it to happen soon.

Just outside the door, she heard footsteps. She stopped moving. She stood dead still, hoping beyond hope that whoever it was wasn't coming to the bathroom. Then the steps stopped just outside the door, and she waited for the handle to tug or at least a knock. There was nothing, though, and then the steps continued, fading down the hall.

Again she was digging into herself, really needing to hurry things up now. But her orgasm was still some ways away, and she knew that she would need to concentrate hard if she was going to be done quickly.

After an eternity, she knew it was happening. She fell

against the wall of the bathroom, just one finger in herself now, and she literally exploded. Her hand was coated in her juices, and she was impressed with this. She loved that she was able to do this to herself, giving the middle finger to Ivor's middle finger.

She pulled herself together and exited the bathroom. She went to make sure nothing was needed from her in the kitchen and then went to work cleaning the upstairs. She did have work to do, and so she was just going to get on with it, forgetting that he had asked her for a drink.

"So this is where you're hiding," she heard Ivor say as he peeked into one of the guest bedrooms.

"Who says I was hiding..." She asked, fluffing the pillows unnecessarily on the bed.

CHAPTER FOUR

*H*e stepped into the room and closed the door. She heard him lock it. She smiled to herself but then remembered her recent downstairs tryst. She was still wet, the smell of her very presence. But he was already walking towards her, and there was nothing she could do.

Ivor lifted her off the ground and threw her on the bed. He got on top of her quickly and pulled her panties all the way off. Then he removed what remained of her clothing before doing the same with his own.

He sent a finger into her, fast. "Somebody's been a bad girl," he whispered, fingering her.

"Very," she said, encouraging him to add a second finger. He obliged, and with these two fingers now, he did bring her to climax.

Then he was on top of her, spreading her legs with himself. He entered her so quickly she gasped. And then he was thrusting into her, fast and furious, like a man possessed with somewhere be. He had nowhere to be, of course, but everything to prove. He planted himself deep inside her.

His eyes were closed. Her eyes were closed too. They

were connected furiously, Ivor giving each and every shot all the energy he could muster. He was really giving it everything he had. There was no need for this, but he wanted her to know that he was up to the task.

She was nowhere near cumming, having recently had a double orgasm. He was close but not wanting to cum just yet. It was quite the conundrum. Ivor thrust hard a few more times, and then he stopped. He pulled himself from her and kissed her mouth hard. Then he kissed her neck, down on her breasts. He made his way down between her legs and went inside her with his tongue.

Still, she wasn't close to cumming, but what he was doing to her with his mouth was incredible. She opened her legs wider so that he had more place to play. He didn't need much space, but that it was given was certainly appreciated.

"You're very good at this..." She said.

He couldn't respond, his mouth a little occupied. His tongue went deep, and he was licking all the flow emanating from her. She really was flowing, and he was enjoying the sweet juices of her punani. Then he worked his way back up onto her mouth, planting himself inside her as their lips connected.

Ivor wasn't as rigorous with his thrusting anymore. He just gave her long beautiful strokes, enjoying each and every one. He was savoring every moment, and she was enjoying it as much. This was feeling more like lovemaking than hard fucking now.

Underneath him, Melissa felt like if this had, in fact, been a competition, then he had definitely won!

He turned them on their side so that they faced each other. He kept himself inside her, moving in and out of her. Their eyes were still locked on each other, and Ivor was making the most beautiful love to her. Then he rolled on top of her again, and again he was thrusting hard.

Ivor gripped the top of her shoulders hard. He pulled her down as hard, almost as hard as he was going into her. It was supersensual and intensely satisfying for both of them. She was taking his perpetual hammering like a real champ.

When he pulled himself from her, he looked down at where she was quivering between her legs. It was a mixture of sweat and love juice, and she couldn't, even if she wanted to, pull her legs back together. The parts of her that were just nailed to the mattress needed to breathe.

They couldn't say much. They didn't need to say much because Ivor's mouth was blowing hot and cold on her special place, trying in vain to make her feel a little better. He was really destroying Melissa now, and so these intermissions were necessary.

He kissed her bottom lips tenderly, thanking her for being as accommodating as she had been. He licked a bit, sent his tongue in just a bit, and then blew hot air all over the outside of her. Then he couldn't hold himself back anymore, and he was back inside her.

Melissa's hands gripped his chest hard as he hammered into her. He was morphing between making it about her and needing to make it about himself. The climax was never his endgame, but it was needed soon. So he just slowed down his strokes, but he didn't make them any less intense and aggressive.

"Stop..." She whispered.

He did, immediately. "Are you okay," he asked.

"I'm fantastic... I just need to breathe... just for a minute!"

Ivor started to pull out. "No..." She said, not wanting him out of her. All she wanted was for him to stop moving.

They were kissing again. Deep passionate kisses that made her forget, for the moment at least, the pleasurable pain she was feeling between her legs. As they kept kissing, deeper, harder, Ivor was again thrusting. His movement inside her was slower, though. He was careful now to make it all about her. He needed to take complete care of her before he could take care of himself.

If he was lucky, he thought, she would take care of him if he did good on her. So he made it his absolute mission to do everything in his power to bring her to an epic end, and then, fingers crossed, he would be allowed to get over that wonderful end himself.

He could hope. All he could do was hope, as he kissed her on her neck tenderly while driving himself slowly, very slowly, in and out of her...

CHAPTER FIVE

*I*vor expertly brought her to climax. It was so careful, so considered, that the build-up was incredible. He really took his time with her because he needed to, but also because he really wanted to.

"Thank you..." She said. She was breathless, but she also knew that Ivor needed to cum. She knew he deserved this.

"Thank you... Very very much," he whispered, still thrusting gingerly into her. He wanted to turn her over and reposition her. He wanted to get fuller access than she had already given up, but he knew that she wouldn't have the energy. So, on her back, legs apart, are just the way he was going to reach his own end.

He pulled himself all the way out. Then he went all the way in again, as slowly, before pulling himself from her completely again. Over and over again, he did this, watching her face before looking at her beautiful breasts. He put his mouth on them, one at a time, before kissing her on her lips again.

All the while, he kept inserting himself into her and completely exiting her, over and over again. He wanted to ram into her and end things now, desperately so, but he was biding his time. It would be a sprint to the finish, but the marathon method had worked so well with her that he thought that he, too, would take it easy.

There was something about taking it slow that was very good. It didn't make him feel like he needed to rush anything, mentally at least, but his body was raging for an orgasm. He needed it to happen soon, but he really was willing to wait. Soon, he told himself.

Soon.

Ivor went all in this time, but he didn't pull out. Not this time. He just couldn't. His mind and body had reached the point of manual override where there was just no turning back. He positioned himself on her better, giving himself the hold he needed.

He was moving faster now, really fast. He was so close that he forgot where he was. He certainly didn't forget who he was with, but he needed her to be a trooper now. He would be done soon.

If he could pull himself from her, he would bring himself to an end himself, but he couldn't. He needed the hot tight hole he was now plowing into rather aggressively. He was holding on to her arms so tightly that his fingertips left imprints in the soft flesh.

"I'm almost done..." He promised.

"Take your time," she whispered, not really meaning it.

Ivor came, at last. Rather, he exploded!

This eruption was nothing short of magnificent, but it was unexpected. Slow and steady, he'd been telling himself, slow and steady. Then he mounted her and thrust aggressively, still reminding himself to take it easy. When he couldn't take it anymore, he just went for it, but it was still slow, still measured.

"That was the undeniable fuck of the millennium," he said, his head in her chest, his whole body shaking.

She was glad. That it was over, yes, but more that he had absolutely enjoyed it. She, too, had enjoyed it, of course. There was just something about the way he made love to her and then fucked her and then went back to making love to her again; that was everything.

He pulled out of her and held her to him. He held her close to him, his big arms around her. She felt safe, protected. She also felt something that she hadn't expected... She felt comfortable.

Melissa fell in and out of a deep sleep while Ivor snored softly behind her. He was expectedly exhausted. She tried a few times to break free from his hold and go to her own bedroom, but Ivor refused to let her go. He wanted to keep her near him.

After a few hours, it was clear why, because they were making love again. And this time, like the many times before that day, it was spectacular. She wasn't tired anymore, and Ivor certainly had got his second wind.

"You're good at everything you do, aren't you," he asked.

"I try to be," she said.

"It wasn't a question!"

They made love one more time, and then Ivor turned over and fell asleep. He said nothing, just needing to rest. Melissa slipped out of his bed when she was sure that he was asleep and gathered her clothes, doing the proverbial walk of shame down to her own room.

She needed to shower, and so she did. Then she needed to sleep, to rest up for the next day. She fell asleep with the most beautiful smile on her happy face...

ABOUT THE AUTHOR

Tala Melton is an emerging erotica author of naughty maids and their billionaire bosses.

Readers: I want to expand a few of the stories to see where the characters can be explored further. If there are any of the stories that you would like to read more about again, I'd love to hear from you!

Visit my blog at Tala Melton Blog
Join my newsletter for free exclusive previews Tala Melton Newsletter
Follow me on Twitter at Tala Melton Twitter
Like my page on Facebook at Tala Melton FB

Sign up for Free Stories from Xplicit Press Authors
Xplicit Press Updates
Like Xplicit Press on Facebook
Follow Xplicit Press on Twitter

www.ingramcontent.com/pod-product-compliance
Lightning Source LLC
Chambersburg PA
CBHW020815130626
46554CB00006B/2458